This book belongs to:

_____

The **START** of **SPRING**

FREDERICK WARNE
Published by the Penguin Group
Penguin Group (USA) LLC
375 Hudson Street
New York, New York 10014

USA | Canada | UK | Ireland | Australia | New Zealand | India | South Africa | China

penguin.com
A Penguin Random House Company

ISBN 978-0-7232-8603-5   10 9 8 7 6 5 4 3 2 1

The **START** of
SPRING

F. WARNE & C<u>O</u>

It was the first day of spring. That meant it was party time at Hilltop Farm. Jemima Puddle-duck had laid an egg. "Life's without a care, when spring is in the air!" she sang happily.

"Do I hear the widdle-waddle of duckling feet, Jemima?" asked Mrs. Tiggy-winkle.

"Not yet, but I know my egg will hatch soon," replied Jemima. "Now, excuse me, I must go and check on it."

But when Jemima came back from her coop she was in a feathery flap.

"Oh dear, oh dear, oh dear,"
she squawked.

"My egg is missing!"

Everyone searched high and low for Jemima's egg,
but it was nowhere to be found.

"Feathers and fur!"
quacked Jemima.
"This is a disaster."

"Don't fret, Jemima," Mrs. Tiggy-winkle
reassured her. "We will find it."

Just then, eagle-eyed Peter Rabbit spotted someone scurrying away from the farm. "It looks like that thieving rat, Samuel Whiskers," he told his friends Lily and Benjamin. "I bet he's got something to do with Jemima's missing egg."

Peter had often seen Samuel stealing things from around town, then pretending to find them so that he would get rewarded with cakes! But no one had yet caught him.

"Let's hop to it!"

cried Peter.

"Follow that rat!"

The three rabbits raced off into the woods.

"I was right, it is that sneaky rat!" whispered Peter, when they caught up with Samuel Whiskers. "Let's hide and see what he's up to."

"You stay there!" Samuel snickered, hiding the stolen egg between some stones. The sneaky snatcher was up to his old tricks.

"Jemima Puddle-duck will be so happy when I hand you back, she'll give me a BIG piece of party cake as a reward!"

Samuel was so busy dreaming about cake, he didn't notice Mr. Tod creeping up and snatching the egg.

"What do we have here?" the crafty fox said, licking his lips hungrily.

"A duck egg for lunch? Yes, that will do nicely."

Samuel spun around. "Give it back!" he shouted, jumping up as high as he could. "I stole that egg fair and square. It's mine!"

"Ha, ha! How amusing," sneered Mr. Tod. "A jumping rat."

Determined to get the egg back, Samuel stamped very hard on Mr. Tod's foot.

"YOOOOW! You dirty rat!" screeched Mr. Tod, tossing the egg high into the air!

All Peter, Lily, and Benjamin could do was watch in horror as Jemima's precious egg soared up and over the wall into Mr. McGregor's garden.

"NO!"

yelled Peter, VERY loudly, forgetting he was supposed to be hiding from Samuel and Mr. Tod.

"It's going to break!"

The rabbits did not hear the egg fall. All they heard was Mr. Tod, as he whirled around to face them and bellowed . . .

"PETER RABBIT!"

"Uh-oh!"
gasped Peter.

"Luckily for you, Whiskers,"
Mr. Tod snarled, "I prefer
hunting rabbits to rats."
And with that, he charged toward Peter.

Samuel quickly slunk off to
look for the egg. Meanwhile,
Benjamin and Lily were hiding
behind a bush, out of sight.

"Peter's in real trouble!"
Benjamin whispered. "We have
to do something to help him."

"I've got an idea," announced Lily, reaching into her Just-in-Case Pocket and pulling out a piece of string. She whispered her plan to Benjamin.

Benjamin hopped nervously out of the bushes and stood
shaking with fright in front of Mr. Tod.

"Ah, dessert!"
snarled the fearsome
fox, licking his lips.

While Mr. Tod was distracted, Lily crept up behind him and
tied his feet together with the string.

The famished fox lunged toward Benjamin, but . . .
he couldn't move!

"C'mon. Quickly!" Lily called to Benjamin and Peter.
And the three friends hopped off, leaving Mr. Tod all tied up.

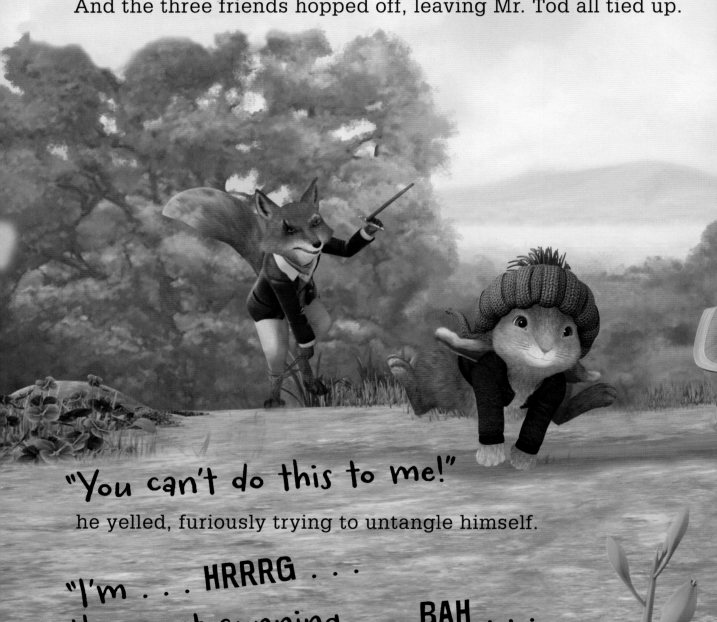

"You can't do this to me!"

he yelled, furiously trying to untangle himself.

"I'm . . . HRRRG . . .
the most cunning . . . BAH . . .
villain in these . . . woods . . ."

"Thanks, guys!" said Peter, relieved to be out of harm's way. "Now, let's find that egg before naughty Samuel Whiskers does."

Peter, Lily, and Benjamin shot down a rabbit hole and away from the very frustrated fox.

The tunnel led straight to Mr. McGregor's garden, where Peter found the egg lying safely on the soft earth.

"We did it!"
cheered Lily.

"We found Jemima's egg before Samuel Whiskers, and it isn't broken."

But just as Peter gently picked up the egg, it began to crack. "Oh no, it's breaking now," said Benjamin anxiously.

"It's not breaking," Lily gasped. "It's hatching! Jemima's duckling is on the way!"

"We'd better get it home to its mommy, and quickly!" cried Peter.

The bunnies hightailed it out of Mr. McGregor's garden
and off toward Hilltop Farm.

But suddenly, Samuel Whiskers jumped out at them and
swiped Jemima's egg right out of Peter's paws!

"Ha, ha, ha," he laughed wickedly.

"I'm going to take this egg back to Jemima and tell everyone that you stole it, Peter! They'll give me a great big piece of cake for saving the day, and you'll be in trouble!"

But Peter, Benjamin, and Lily just smiled . . .

They could see Jemima, and all her friends from the party, standing behind Samuel. They had been looking for the egg and overheard EVERYTHING he had said. They were not happy!

Samuel turned around to face them. "Oh, er. Ahem," he stammered. "You must've . . ."

" . . . heard everything?" finished Jemima Puddle-duck, quacking angrily.

"Yes, we did! What a sneaky rat you are, stealing my egg and trying to blame it on Peter Rabbit!"

Jemima snatched her egg from Samuel, scolding him with a loud and angry, **"QUACK!"** in his ear.

"You'd best run along, Samuel Whiskers," warned Mrs. Tiggy-winkle, pretending to be fierce, "or you'll be feeling the sharp end of my spines, you cheeky egg-stealing rascal!"

So off Samuel skulked into the woods, with no egg and no reward, and his long rat's tail between his legs.

Jemima was just thanking Peter, Lily, and Benjamin for finding the egg before it hatched when . . . **CRRAAAACK!**

Jemima started to flap. "Oh dear, oh dear, oh dear. I think I'm having . . ."

" . . . a duckling!" she cried, just as a beautiful, fluffy yellow duckling hatched from the egg and waddled out of its shell with a tiny little, "QUACK!"

Everyone smiled at the gorgeous baby duck.

"Now I hear the widdle-waddle of duckling feet!" Mrs. Tiggy-winkle laughed. "Congratulations, Jemima!"

"Why, thank you, Mrs. Tiggy-winkle," replied a very proud Jemima Puddle-duck.

"Let's go back to the farm and celebrate!" cried Lily excitedly.

Snuggling close her precious bundle, Jemima led everyone
back to Hilltop Farm.

"I say we get this spring party started,"
she cheered.

Jeremy Fisher sang a happy spring song, and all the woodland
friends danced together around the fuzzy little duckling.

Everyone was so happy that springtime had sprung
and new life had begun . . .

Everyone, that was, except
for sulky Samuel Whiskers!